The Invisible Castle

A THRILLER

By Les Martin

Illustrated by Esteban Maroto

Adapted from the teleplay by Peter Lawrence

D0205066

Random House New York

Library of Congress Cataloging-in-Publication Data: Martin, Les, 1934—. The invisible
castle. On t.p. the registered trademark symbol "TM" is superscript following
"Thundercats" in the title. SUMMARY: Lion-O experiences dangerous adventures when
he goes to the rescue of Jaga, fellow Thundercat held prisoner in a castle in the Astral
World. [1. Fantasy] I. Maroto, Esteban, ill. II. Lawrence, Peter. Astral prison.
III. Title. PZ7.M36353Io 1986 [Fic] 85-19649 ISBN: 0-394-87878-7

Manufactured in the United States of America 1 2 3 4 5 6 7 8 9 0

Contents

1

Growl of Warning

A powerful catlike growl thundered from the Sword Chamber of the Cats' Lair, home of the Thundercats on Third Earth.

When Lion-O heard it, his magnificently muscled body tensed and his handsome face became serious and intent. Swiftly the Thundercats' leader moved to the secret panel that concealed the device to open the Sword Chamber door.

The door swung open. Lion-O blinked, half blinded, as dazzling light met his eyes.

When they adjusted, he entered the Sword

Chamber and went directly to the source of the sound and the light: the Sword of Omens.

The Sword was Lion-O's servant in battle. But at times like this it was his master, summoning him with its thunderous growl.

The Sword was growling more loudly now than it ever had before. Just below its hilt, the Eye of Thundera was ablaze with light.

Lion-O picked up the Sword and gazed into the all-seeing Eye.

The moment he did so, the growling faded and the light dimmed. And what Lion-O saw and heard in the Eye of Thundera made him eager to take the Sword in his fighting hand and go into battle.

The first thing that Lion-O saw was a strange castle of crystal, surrounded by a silvery, mirrorlike moat. The castle looked as solid as rock yet as transparent as glass.

What an eerie place, Lion-O thought, a chill running through him. *It looks like it was made to house ghosts.*

Then the castle faded and a prison cell

took its place. In the center of the cell was a tiny, wizened creature who looked as ghostly as the castle. Light seeped through his skin as if his flesh were no more solid than smoke. But the long claws on his hands and feet were real enough. So were his three green glowing eyes, and his cloak studded with jewels of the same glowing green.

There was another figure in the cell, and when Lion-O saw him, he gasped in surprise and dismay. "Jaga!"

Jaga was the wisest of all Thundercats, the one on whom all the other Thundercats depended in times of doubt and indecision. Then Jaga would come to them from where he dwelled in the realm of the invisible to light their way.

But now it was Jaga who needed help.

He was chained to the cell wall, and the creature who was his captor was crowing, "I have planned this moment for years! I, Nemex, warden of the Astral Prison, have you, Jaga, as my prisoner—for all eternity!"

That was enough for Lion-O. A growl rose in his throat. Sword in hand, he raced out of the room. As soon as he was through the door, his voice thundered through the Cats' Lair.

"Thundercats, assemble in the Council Chamber Room! Immediately!"

His words had instant effect. All the other

Thundercats—Panthro, Tygra, Cheetara, Snarf, even the mischievous Wilykit and Wilykat—dropped what they were doing and headed for the council room.

But his words had another effect as well. An effect Lion-O certainly did not intend. And could not suspect.

2

Witch's Brew

In a distant part of Third Earth, far from the Cats' Lair, lightning flashed. High in the air, the lightning divided itself into four jagged fingers. They reached down to touch the four needlelike black obelisks around the Black Pyramid of Mumm-Ra, then shot to the top of the pyramid and penetrated to its core, where the tomb of Mumm-Ra was hidden.

The statues of hideous man-beasts guarding the tomb glowed. Then from the tomb an even more hideous figure emerged.

It was Mumm-Ra, roused from his endless

sleep of undying evil. Clothed in a flapping cloak, with his bandages sagging loosely around his withered body, he shuffled to the bubbling cauldron nearby.

"That bolt of warning lightning was most powerful," he muttered. "There must be very unusual activity in the Cats' Lair. What are those cursed Thundercats up to now?"

Mumm-Ra peered into the steam rising from the cauldron and watched with interest as the steam turned into a picture of the Thundercats gathered in the Cats' Lair.

His ancient eyes gleamed. What were they doing? What evil could he work on them . . . ?

In the Council Chamber Room, Lion-O surveyed the other Thundercats at the council table.

Tygra, cool and clearheaded, carrying the weighted whip that was his favorite weapon.

Cheetara, beautiful, bold and swift, gifted with second sight and armed with her magic staff.

Panthro, the strongest of them all, and the hottest-tempered, like a volcano always ready to erupt.

Wilykit and Wilykat, young and sometimes foolish, but always ready to do their part in battle with their lariats and smoke pellets.

And last and most lovable, Snarf, as brave as he was bumbling.

Satisfied that they all were paying attention, Lion-O announced, "Jaga has been captured! He's a prisoner in a castle in the Astral World!"

"The Astral World?" said Wilykit.

"Sounds like some sort of fun park," said Wilykat.

"This is no joking matter," said Lion-O, in a tone that made the rambunctious pair fall silent instantly. "The Astral World is the invisible world that Jaga lives in. It is as close to us as the air against our skins. Yet it is as distant as the farthest reaches of space."

"How do you find it—if you can't see it?" asked Wilykit.

"Is there a map or something?" added Wilykat.

"I wish there were," said Lion-O. "Even more, I wish I had the wisdom of Jaga to

guide me to it. But this is one time he can't come to my aid. I have to go to his." He turned to Cheetara. "Maybe your second sight can help me."

Cheetara's slanting eyes narrowed. But she had to shake her head. "It's no use. I can pick up vibrations from things in this world. But not in the other one."

"There is someone—or maybe I should say some*thing*—who knows much about the Astral World," said Tygra thoughtfully. "I hesitate to mention the name though."

"Who is it?" asked Lion-O.

"The Netherwitch," said Tygra.

"The Netherwitch!" said Wilykat with a grimace.

"Ughh," said Wilykit. "Who would go to *her*?"

"If it were the only way to save Jaga," said Lion-O, "I'd go to the Devil himself!"

That was all that Mumm-Ra had to see and hear to make him rub his twisted hands together in glee.

"So Lion-O wants to see the Netherwitch,"

he cackled. "So he shall. So he shall."

Mumm-Ra held out his scrawny arms, and a voice that seemed too large for his body boomed out of his mouth.

"Ancient spirits of evil, transform this decayed form into Mumm-Ra the Ever-Living!"

As he spoke, his appearance changed. By the time he gave the last word of his command, the change was complete. He stood tall and straight, his muscles bulging under his outspread cape.

But he was not yet finished.

"And now the sorceress of the Netherworld!"

And in the place of Mumm-Ra the Ever-Living stood the ravishing, green-eyed Netherwitch, grand mistress of black magic.

She laughed softly. In a voice as smooth as a silken noose she said, "Lion-O won't know that Mumm-Ra and the Netherwitch are one and the same—until it's too late."

3

The Jaws of Danger

"Good-bye, my friends," said Lion-O to the other Thundercats. He got out of the ThunderTank and looked out over the swirling River of Despair. Beyond the river was the Pit of the Netherwitch. "I have a hunch the Mutants are planning trouble," he added. "Be on your guard. They've been too quiet lately."

"Don't worry about us—we'll be ready if they try anything," said Panthro, sitting at the controls of the ThunderTank. As always, the thought of combat made him glow with something close to joy. "Worry about yourself. Are you sure you want to see the Netherwitch alone? I'll gladly go with you."

"You're needed to help defend the Cats' Lair," said Lion-O. "The Sword of Omens will give me all the help I need."

"I hope you're right," said Cheetara, "and that you're not facing a force that even the Sword can't defeat."

"I *know* I'm right. The Sword has never failed me yet," said Lion-O, and with the Sword he motioned for the ThunderTank to depart.

Smiling, he waved good-bye as the ThunderTank roared away. But his smile faded as he turned to face the river between him and the Pit of the Netherwitch.

There's just one way across, he thought with a shudder. *The Bridge of Slime.*

Come on, you can do it. You have *to do it— Jaga needs you,* he told himself as he gazed at the bridge. It looked like a huge bent tree trunk that arched from one bank of the river to the other. But it was not made of wood. It

17

was made of a substance as smooth and slippery as ice, and covered by a dripping coat of slime.

This is a job for the Claw Shield, thought Lion-O. The shield, an ingenious glove-shaped device tipped with metal claws, often served Lion-O as a weapon. Now he had another use for it.

Fighting his queasiness, he lay stomach down on the bridge with his legs dangling down on either side. He dug the Claw Shield into the bridge and pulled himself forward. Inch by inch, foot by foot, he slid along the slimy surface, leaving one riverbank behind and straining to reach the other.

He was halfway across when a snapping sound made him look down.

Directly below him a monstrous head was emerging from the water. Its huge jaws snapped a few inches from his dangling feet.

A Gaw Rak-Rak, Lion-O thought, and reached for his sword. *I'll soon take care of youououou . . .*

His thoughts of attacking the river monster

vanished as he felt himself sliding off the bridge.

The Gaw Rak-Rak's eyes gleamed ravenously, and it shot out of the water to snatch the coming feast.

By now Lion-O's Claw Shield had lost its grip. He was falling toward his doom.

Then his sword hand went to action.

Desperately he plunged the Sword of Omens into the bridge, so that it stuck straight out of the side. Gripping the Sword, his powerful arm muscles bulging, he swung back and forth while the sharp-toothed jaws below snapped and snarled in futile pursuit of his swinging feet.

With a final mighty heave, Lion-O swung himself back onto the bridge. Lying there on his stomach, breathing hard, he retrieved the Sword and returned it to its scabbard.

As Lion-O resumed his progress toward the safety of the shore, the Gaw Rak-Rak growled in frustration.

Within the scabbard, the Sword of Omens growled too.

"Don't worry, Sword," Lion-O said. "I know the shore isn't safe. And I know I have to be on the lookout for danger when I go down into the Pit of the Netherwitch."

But Lion-O did not suspect what kind of danger was waiting for him in the pit.

And what kind of danger was brewing in another place as well—threatening not him but all the other Thundercats.

4

A Pair of Perils

The ugly sound of loud Mutant laughter rang off the walls of the fortress called Castle Plun-Darr. Here S-S-Slithe, Jackalman, Monkian, and Vultureman, bitter enemies of the Thundercats, were happily congratulating themselves.

They were in Vultureman's workshop, inspecting the weapon they had helped him build.

"S-s-splendid work," said S-S-Slithe. The toothlike spikes running down his back quivered with pleasure. "A Thundranium cannon, able to shoot Thundranium shells."

"Thundranium—the only thing that can weaken those dratted Thundercats," said Vultureman. His beady eyes glittered as he gazed at the gleaming new cannon. It had four rapid-fire barrels and was mounted on wheels for easy transport. Right next to it was stacked a towering supply of Thundranium shells. Brightly colored—red, blue, orange, green, yellow, purple—they looked like a rainbow *before* a storm.

"I can't wait to fire them into the Cats' Lair," exulted Monkian, jumping up and down with jabbering apelike joy.

Vultureman patted the cannon. "This is our greatest chance ever to destroy them once and for all—especially since Lion-O won't be there to defend them with his cursed sword."

"*If* he won't be there," said Jackalman, his snout quivering with suspicion.

"Why should Mumm-Ra lie to us?" said S-S-Slithe. "It is not in his-s-s interest. I am sure that at this-s-s very minute, Lion-O is walking straight into Mumm-Ra's trap."

S-S-Slithe was wrong. Lion-O wasn't *walking* into Mumm-Ra's trap. He was *sliding* into it, down the sloping sides of the Pit of the Netherwitch.

It was the only way Lion-O could see to descend into the pit. Too late, he discovered that its sides were covered with the same slick slime that coated the bridge he had crossed. By that time he was sliding out of control.

Slam! Lion-O hit the bottom and lay there stunned. Shaking his head groggily, he got to his feet and pulled out the Sword of Omens.

"Guide me, Sword," he said. Light shot from its tip, and he saw the entrance to a tunnel.

Lion-O entered, with the Sword lighting his way through the dank darkness.

"Wha . . . ?" said Lion-O, startled, freezing in his tracks. In front of him was a laughing, three-eyed demon's face.

Lion-O raised the Sword to defend himself, only to be grabbed by glowing ghostly hands.

He slashed at them with the Sword. But

the Sword passed through them as if they were ghostly visions.

Their grip on Lion-O, though, was as strong as steel. He was helpless as they held him—and helpless as they hurled him into the gaping hole that yawned at his feet.

He fell. And fell. And fell. Through empty space. For what seemed like forever. And then—nothingness.

Lion-O did not know how long he lay there. He only knew that when he came to, he was still clutching the Sword of Omens.

But the beautiful, green-eyed woman who stood looking down at him showed no fear of it.

Her blood-red lips parted in a smile as white and cold as virgin snow.

"So, Lord of the Thundercats, you want to enter the Astral World to free Jaga?"

Lion-O shook his head to clear it as he got to his feet.

"How . . . how did you know that?"

"I am the Netherwitch, Lion-O. I know everything."

Unsteadily Lion-O faced her. He still could not throw off the shock of his fall, though he knew he had to—fast. He felt the force coming from this raven-haired sorceress—a force even more powerful than the ghostly hands that had hurled him into these depths where she dwelled.

He felt as if he were in a wrestling match with her—and was being forced further and further off balance.

But he could not afford to break contact. He needed her help too badly.

"Will you help me?" he asked. "Can you get me into the Astral World?"

"Of course, dear Lion-O," said the Netherwitch sweetly. "But once you are there, you can never return."

"But . . ." said Lion-O, frantically trying to think straight. There had to be some kind of bargain he could strike. There had to be. . . .

"*No! Never!* Choose now—or lose your chance *forever!*" the Netherwitch spat out, swiftly as a serpent striking.

"I have to free Jaga . . ." Lion-O said, thinking out loud.

"This is the only way to do it," the Netherwitch replied.

Still Lion-O hesitated. How could he trust this creature?

But how could he argue with her?

Jaga's freedom was at stake.

And she was offering the only way to free him.

"You agree to go?" demanded the Netherwitch, pushing him to his decision.

"I agree to go," said Lion-O.

That was all the Netherwitch had to hear. Her voice rose in a cackle of triumph. "Ancient Spirits of the Void . . . transport Lion-O . . . to the Astral World!"

As she spoke, the form of Lion-O faded. And as he faded, the Netherwitch changed.

The last thing Lion-O saw before he vanished from Third Earth was the form of Mumm-Ra the Ever-Living, taking the place of the Netherwitch.

And his last thought was, *I've been tricked!*

5

Astral Action

At least the Eye of Thundera wasn't playing tricks, Lion-O thought as he gazed at the Astral Prison.

He was standing at the edge of the silvery moat that surrounded the crystal castle he had seen in the Eye. It was exactly as the Eye had pictured it, though now he could see more of the world around it.

The castle was in the middle of a desert that stretched to the horizon on all sides. Lion-O blinked as he tried to take in that vast and bleak expanse. In the eerie light that

29

flooded this world, hills and valleys merged and melted, flowed and froze, in ever-shifting patterns. He could not tell what was near and what was far away, and the more he looked, the less he saw.

This would be an easy world to get lost in, he thought. *Good thing I know where I'm going. Across the moat and into the castle to rescue Jaga. And good thing I know how to get there.*

Lion-O took his Claw Shield from his belt and set its firing device. He aimed the shield at the castle and pulled the trigger.

A line with a claw at its tip sped through the air and hooked on to the top of the castle wall.

"Bull's-eye!" said Lion-O as he swung himself across the moat and began to haul himself up the outside of the wall.

Moments later he was standing on the castle parapet. "That was the easy part," he said, looking down the steep crystal stairway that led inside the castle. "Now it gets tough."

The stairway was brightly lit, but the light

of the Astral World only lit the way to confusion, masking distances and twisting shapes. Lion-O had to descend the stairs one careful step at a time, unable to see when they treacherously slanted sharply or shortened suddenly. And when he reached the bottom of the stairs, his path was even more bewildering.

The crystal corridors that he moved through looked perfectly straight. But he quickly found that they swerved right and left and up and down. Lion-O bumped into wall after wall. Time after time he lost his balance. His feet stumbled, his senses swam.

Then, from behind a locked door in a corridor lined with locked doors, he heard a voice that made him freeze in place and made his mind icy clear.

And when he looked in through the window that was set in that door, what he saw made his blood boil.

6

Fight for Freedom

Nemex, warden of the Astral Prison, was just as hideous in person as he had looked in the Eye of Thundera. Tiny and wizened, he had claws on his hands and feet, and a rasping voice that snarled at Jaga, "Only when you surrender all of your knowledge will I consider freeing you!"

Jaga's aged muscles were not strong enough to break the chains that bound him to the cell wall. But the strength of his ageless spirit was as strong as ever.

"Never will I give that knowledge to a

33

creature like you, Nemex," he replied.

Nemex laughed scornfully. "Brave words, feeble fool. But I, Nemex, master of all who are captive in the Astral World, have eternity to change your mind. And, my poor Jaga, you can be sure I have the means to do it."

Nemex's laughter rose even higher—until a voice from outside the cell rose above it.

"Not if I have anything to do with it, Nemex."

"Who *dares*—?" Nemex began, then saw Lion-O's angry face through the cell door window.

For a split second Nemex shrank back. Then his voice swelled. "You think you can overcome me, intruder? I will make you see differently!"

As he spoke, green beams of light shot out from his eyes, and his body shot up, doubling in height.

In answer, Lion-O ran full force at the cell door and crashed through it in a shower of crystal splinters—to find himself facing a massively muscled, cruelly smiling giant.

Lion-O ducked the green beams shooting

from Nemex's eyes. They singed the top of his red mane of hair and burned black holes in the wall behind him.

"Try again, Nemex," mocked Lion-O.

"I will—and this time I'll get you!" screamed Nemex. His huge arms thrust out toward Lion-O, and the long claws on his fingers pointed straight at Lion-O's heart.

"Burn!" roared Nemex, and ten beams of yellow light shot from his fingers.

Instantly Jaga shouted from where he was chained, "The Eye of Thundera, Lion-O! *Use its power!*"

His words came not a moment too soon. Lion-O had just enough time to raise the Sword of Omens in front of him, holding it so that the Eye of Thundera shielded his heart.

"Grrrrrrr." The Sword sounded its battle growl as the beams hit the Eye.

"Aghhhhhhh!" shrieked Nemex in agony as the ten bright beams turned into one blinding shaft of light in the Eye of Thundera and came blazing back at him.

"*Noooo. . . .*" Nemex moaned as the beam flared in a gigantic yellow fireball around him, and his body shriveled back to its former pitiful size.

Lion-O stepped forward, seized the tiny Nemex by the front of his cloak, and lifted him into the air.

Hissing, Nemex tried to claw his way loose, but his feeble attempts only made Lion-O's grin wider.

"Stop that, little man," Lion-O said, "or I'll toss you into your own moat."

Still holding Nemex in one hand, Lion-O turned to Jaga.

"Thank you for saving me once again with your wisdom," he said. "Now it is my turn to save you."

With his free hand, Lion-O used his sheer strength to snap the chains that bound Jaga to the wall. Then, tossing Nemex like a rag doll into a corner of the cell, Lion-O used both hands to tear apart the chains around Jaga's wrists and ankles.

"Thank you, Lion-O," said Jaga. Those

simple words were all the reward that Lion-O could want. And Jaga's next words made him glow. "I am glad to see you are making progress in mastering your own strength and the power of the Sword."

"You'll never get away with this!" croaked Nemex from the corner.

"With the Sword in my hand, and Jaga at my side, nothing can stop me," said Lion-O.

"We'll see about that," said Nemex. He put all his remaining power into a high-pitched scream: *"Guards!"*

"Guess it's time to say good-bye, Nemex," said Lion-O as he and Jaga headed out through the shattered cell door.

"I'll lead the way," said Jaga as they moved down the crystal corridor. The tricks that the astral light played could not trick him. He saw through them as he saw through all deceptions.

"With you in charge, we'll be out of this castle in no time," said Lion-O.

"But even I don't know how to get you out of the Astral World," Jaga told him. "I, who am more spirit than flesh, can return to Third Earth with ease when I am needed. But you have not yet reached that higher stage of being."

"We'll worry about that later," Lion-O said. "First we have to escape the guards. Nemex sounded as if he has an army of them."

"He has—and they are armed with weapons more menacing—and magic more powerful—than any on Third Earth," said Jaga. "Even I was not able to withstand his guards when they surrounded me and made me prisoner."

They both quickened their pace, running at full speed through the maze of corridors.

Then came a sound that stopped them in their tracks.

It was the one sound that could stop them—the sound of a voice crying "Help me!"

7

The Eye of Doom

The voice crying for help came from behind a locked door, a door that Lion-O blasted open instantly with a beam from his sword.

Cautiously he and Jaga entered the room, fearing a trap. But they relaxed when they saw who had called out to them.

He was ancient beyond calculation. His long red hair and immense tangle of red beard had gone countless years without cutting. Only one eye remained to him, and even that was dim. But it shone with joy when he saw Lion-O and Jaga.

"Rescued at last," he said in a quavering voice as Lion-O took him by the arm and raised him up.

"Thank you, my boy," the ancient man said. "I will reward your kindness."

Lion-O smiled at the idea of this frail figure helping *him*. Then his smile faded as he heard the distant shouts and running footsteps of approaching guards. Lion-O swept the ancient man up in his arms, and he and Jaga ran for their lives.

"This way!" said Jaga, and led them into a corridor that plunged them into pitch darkness.

Wondering where they were, Lion-O tucked the ancient man under one arm and drew his sword with his free hand. He sent a beam of light through the darkness and saw that the sides and roof of the corridor were beaded with drops of water.

"We're in a tunnel that leads under the moat," said Jaga. "It was built to be an emergency exit—and it's our only way out."

"You mean, it *was* our only way out," said

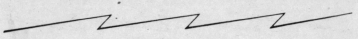

Lion-O as the light beam shone on a wall that blocked off the tunnel.

"Nemex must have built that wall to seal off all escape," said Jaga.

"He thought of everything," said Lion-O, "except *this*."

The light beam changed to a laser beam, and the wall crumbled away.

"Easy as pie," said Lion-O.

"Except for one thing," said Jaga, and pointed upward.

Cracks were spreading through the tunnel ceiling.

"The wall must have acted as a support," said Lion-O.

"Run!" commanded Jaga.

They leaped over the rubble and dashed down the tunnel. Behind them came the roar of water rushing through the collapsing ceiling. Then, ahead of them, a dot of light appeared, growing larger with every racing step.

Their last steps were taken sloshing through knee-deep water. They flung themselves out of the tunnel and lay panting by the exit. The tunnel came out behind a large

rock that shielded them from view of the castle.

"Nemex will figure we drowned," Lion-O said. "We're safe—for a while at least." Then he heard the Sword of Omens begin to growl. "Or maybe we aren't. Let's see how close the danger is." He looked into the Eye of Thundera.

But the danger he saw wasn't close at all. It was far away—painfully far away.

On Third Earth.

At the Cats' Lair.

Vultureman, happy as a child with a new toy, fired his cannon at the Cats' Lair. Shells of Thundranium, a rare element, crashed into the lair, spreading clouds of Thundranium particles. Vultureman laughed. Thundranium sapped the strength of even the strongest Thundercat. Soon they would all be too weak to defend themselves.

Meanwhile, S-S-Slithe's face was split by a malicious grin as he drove his Nosediver toward the Cats' Lair, its guns blazing.

At the same time, Monkian and Jackalman swooped down from the air in their Sky-Cutters like savage birds of prey, spitting out destruction with their cannons.

But the Thundercats were not giving up.

With the Cat's Eyes' lasers, Panthro and Cheetara returned the SkyCutters' fire.

"Got one," Panthro growled. His eyes were fiery as he saw Monkian's SkyCutter burst into flame and go into a nosedive.

"Drat," Panthro muttered when Monkian regained control of the craft just before crashing and returned to the fight.

"I'll get you this time," said Panthro, zeroing in on the speeding speck.

But at that moment his attention was diverted by news of a greater threat.

"Those are Thundranium shells they're firing into here," said Cheetara, examining the smoking shells embedded in the walls. Inside the Cats' Lair, the different colors of the smoke mingled to form a black haze—the color of death.

"Check the Thundranium level," Tygra

told Wilykit, who had the Thundranium counter.

"It's 129 — and rising fast," reported Wilykit.

Wilykat looked over his shoulder and confirmed the report with a vigorous nod.

For once neither of the youngsters was playing around.

"If it rises much higher, we're done for," said Tygra.

"We have to knock out that cannon," said Panthro. "I'm taking the ThunderTank and going after it."

"I'll go with you," declared Snarf, his roly-

poly body quivering with determination.

Even at this grim moment, the Thunder-cats had to grin at the idea of gentle, bumbling Snarf going into battle.

"I think you'd better keep on guarding the home front," said Panthro.

"We wouldn't feel safe here without you," said Cheetara, patting Snarf on the shoulder.

"Well, if you say so," said Snarf reluctantly.

"Don't worry, I can do the job myself," said Panthro. As always, he was eager for action. He pressed the starter of the ThunderTank, its engine roared, and he waited impatiently for the great stone paws of the Cats' Lair to come up. As they did a bridge extended out of the lair, and Panthro was on his way.

"Up and at 'em!" he shouted, heading out to where the Mutant menace waited.

"If anyone can do it, he can," said Wilykat bravely.

But Wilykit said what all the Thundercats were thinking: "If only Lion-O and the Sword of Omens were here."

8

Help!

"If only I were there," groaned Lion-O as he looked into the Eye of Thundera and saw the battle at the Cats' Lair unfold.

The Sword of Omens growled in agreement.

But they were both helpless. The best they could do was to wait and see what happened when Panthro attacked.

Vultureman waited, too, as Panthro came at him in the ThunderTank.

But Vultureman *could* do something.

Expertly he spun the controls of the Thundranium cannon to adjust its elevation. Carefully he squinted through its sights. And with a smile he pressed its firing button.

One after another, the four cannon barrels pumped shells into the ThunderTank.

The ThunderTank shuddered like a wounded animal and veered out of control. Then, when the fourth shell hit it, it tipped over on its side and lay with one of its treads spinning in air.

Airborne in his SkyCutter, Jackalman enjoyed a bird's-eye view of Panthro crawling from the wrecked ThunderTank. "Now for the kill!" Jackalman cried.

The SkyCutter came down, guns blazing. But the moment Panthro was free of the ThunderTank, he used all his enormous muscle power for a lightning-fast zigzag run to the Cats' Lair. Bullets kicked up dust all around him, but none hit his darting, dodging form.

Angrily Jackalman had to pull up from his dive.

"I'll get him next time," he snarled. "He'll never make it back to the lair." A loud, steady booming told him that the cannon had resumed its bombardment of the trapped Thundercats. "Besides, soon there won't be a Cats' Lair to go back to, hnyah, hnyah!"

In the Astral World, Lion-O lowered the Eye of Thundera. He could stand to watch no more.

"The Cats' Lair is being destroyed—and I'm stuck here," he groaned. "Are you *sure* you can't get me back to Third Earth, Jaga?"

Jaga shook his head.

"Then no one can help me—or any of the other Thundercats," Lion-O said despairingly.

"*I* can help you."

For a moment Lion-O did not know where the powerful voice came from. Then he realized it came from the frail ancient man he had rescued.

"*You?*" said Lion-O. "How could *you* help *us*?"

"My name is Brodo," the ancient one said. "Centuries ago I was the greatest magician on Third Earth. My wizardry threatened Mumm-Ra's evil power. He disguised himself as the beautiful Netherwitch, tricked me, and trapped me in the Astral Prison."

"Sounds familiar," said Lion-O.

"Inside the prison walls I was powerless— but now my powers have returned," Brodo said. "Now you can be my instrument of vengeance on him and his Mutant allies—if you're willing to do battle with them."

"I'm more than willing," said Lion-O.

"Then get your sword ready for action," said Brodo.

"And prepare your spirit as well," said Jaga.

"Right," said Lion-O. He felt the power of the Sword in his hand. And he felt a different kind of strength as well—a strength that filled him as if from a calm wellspring in his innermost being.

Brodo pointed his fingers at Lion-O.

Those fingers grew long and youthful as

Brodo said, "Ancient Spirits of Good . . . transport Lion-O . . . back to his own world!"

As Brodo spoke, he and Jaga faded away. When his last word of command died in the air, the entire Astral World had vanished, and Lion-O was moving with meteoric speed through vast empty space. And all he could think was, *Will I get there in time?*

9

Sword in the Sky

"It's all over," gasped Cheetara weakly as the laser gun fell from her hand. The Thundranium smoke filling the fortress room of the Cats' Lair had done its evil work: it had sapped the strength of the Thundercats and left them powerless. They had been struggling to fight on, but with each passing moment their efforts grew feebler. Using her last ounce of strength, Cheetara raised herself to look out the window. Far below she saw Panthro making a desperate run toward the lair. Above him, in their SkyCutters,

Jackalman and Monkian were poised to zoom in and destroy him, cheered on by S-S-Slithe in his Nosediver and Vultureman at his booming cannon.

Cheetara's heart sank:

Then suddenly the cannon went silent.

The Nosediver skidded to a halt.

The SkyCutters hung motionless in the air.

Panthro stopped running.

And Cheetara cheered with all the strength left in her.

In the sky above the battlefield the Sword of Omens had appeared—a thousand times larger than life.

Then, as all below watched in wonderment, a huge hand appeared to grip it.

Next an immense arm became visible.

And finally in the sky a giant Lion-O armed with the Sword of Omens was there for everyone to see.

"Lion-O and the Sword have returned!" exclaimed Cheetara. The strength of new hope filled her and the other Thundercats. They clustered around her at the window to watch Lion-O and the Sword slowly descend to earth.

As Lion-O and the Sword came closer to landing, they gradually returned to their normal sizes.

"I was scared for a moment there," Vultureman said with a sneer from behind his Thundranium cannon. "But you're not too big for me to handle now, Lion-O."

With feverish speed, he lined up Lion-O in the cannon sights.

But then he saw something that froze his finger on the firing button.

Lion-O was hurling the Sword directly at the cannon.

Crackling with ferocious energy, the Sword flew through the air and straight into the first cannon barrel set to fire. There was an ear-splitting *bang!* as it met the nose of the emerging shell, and then an explosion of bright green smoke.

Thrown backward ten feet, Vultureman watched the smoke settle. "My beautiful cannon," he moaned.

All that remained of the mighty Thundranium cannon was a heap of jagged, twisted metal. Gleaming on top of it, completely unharmed, lay the Sword of Omens.

Lion-O raced to retrieve the Sword—but S-S-Slithe, in the Nosediver, cut off his path.

"Got you now, Lion-O," he hissed from his deadly armored vehicle. "You're defenseless without your cursed s-s-sword."

He aimed the pointed nose and powerful guns of the Nosediver directly at Lion-O.

"Time to s-s-say good-bye, Lion-O," he said with a sneer—and then his mouth fell open. Violent explosions shook the Nose-diver, spinning it halfway around on its treads.

S-S-Slithe could guess what those explosions meant.

"Panthro—and his infernal nunchaku," he hissed.

He was right. Panthro was back on the attack, coming to Lion-O's rescue with the awesome explosive pellets that were his favorite weapon.

"Got to get away," muttered S-S-Slithe. But it wouldn't be easy. Before he could stop the Nosediver, it was plunging straight ahead—into a cloud of thick, choking black smoke.

S-S-Slithe had not seen Wilykit and Wilykat emerging from the Cats' Lair to hurl smoke bombs at the Nosediver. And he could not see the crater he drove into with a bone-jarring crash—until he hit the bottom.

But Monkian and Jackalman in their

SkyCutters above could see it all: the destroyed Thundranium cannon, the wrecked Nosediver, and the Thundercats recovering from the weakening effects of Thundranium and back in fighting form.

Both Mutants had the same thought at the same time.

"Let's get out of here!"

But Cheetara had already hurled her magic staff at Jackalman's SkyCutter.

The staff flew through the air as straight as an arrow shot from a powerful bow. And as it flew it lengthened and picked up speed.

Jackalman had only time to gasp "Hnyah, hnyah, hnyah" before the staff hit his SkyCutter and sent it into a twisting tailspin. The craft smashed into a treetop and hung in pieces from the branches while Jackalman climbed out and jumped to the ground. Whimpering, he staggered to his feet and started to run.

Monkian had no better luck when he tried to dodge the bola whip that Tygra hurled up at him. Balls of fire flared from the bola's tips as they hit the Mutant's SkyCutter. A minute later the SkyCutter's nose was buried in the ground, and a jibbering Monkian was limping away. Soon he joined the other Mutants fleeing the scene of their failure and the Thundercats' triumph.

61

10

"Hooray for Team Thundercat!"

Lion-O, Sword in hand, stood with the other Thundercats and watched the pitiful figures of the Mutants scurrying away.

"They'll think twice before attacking the Cats' Lair again," he said.

"If they had any brains to think with, they wouldn't have tried it at all," said Tygra with a grin.

"They must have thought that Lion-O and the Sword wouldn't be here to save us," said Cheetara. "Thank you, Lion-O."

"It's I who should thank you—for saving

me just now," said Lion-O, and the Sword of Omens growled in agreement.

Then they heard a voice. Jaga's voice.

"That is the way to win," he said. "Not fighting alone, but as a team."

Lion-O and the other Thundercats nodded solemnly. With Lion-O leading the way, they formed a circle and raised their clasped hands high.

"Hooray for Team Thundercat!" shouted Wilykat.

"Hooray for us all!" Wilykit echoed.

And Lion-O knew that Jaga, from wherever he watched over them, was cheering too.